ANYTHING CAN HAPPEN,
YOU JUST HAVE TO BELIEVE!

Minerva Mint

capstone
young readers

Minerva Mint is published by Capstone Young Readers
A Capstone Imprint
1710 Roe Crest Drive
North Mankato, Minnesota 56003
www.capstoneyoungreaders.com

Text by Elisa Puricelli Guerra; Translated by Chiara Pernigotti
Original edition published by Edizioni Piemme S.p.A., Italy
Original title: La leggenda del pirata Black Bart

International Rights © Atlantyca S.p.A., via Leopardi 8 - 20123 Milano – Italia —
foreignrights@atlantyca.it — www.atlantyca.com

Library of Congress Cataloging-in-Publication Data is available
on the Library of Congress website.

ISBN: 978-1-6237-0068-3 (hardcover)
ISBN: 978-1-4342-6512-8 (library binding)
ISBN: 978-1-4342-6515-9 (paperback)

Summary:
Was the late Black Bart so mean that his spirit cannot find peace? Minerva and friends will
find out!

Designer:
Veronica Scott

Printed in China by Nordica.
1013/CA21301908
092013   007736NORDS14

THE LEGEND OF BLACK BART

by Elisa Puricelli Guerra

illustrated by Gabo León Bernstein

TABLE OF CONTENTS

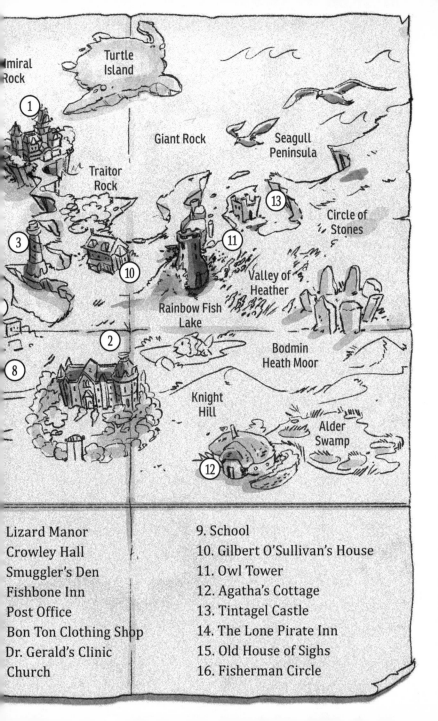

WHAT'S HAPPENED SO FAR . . .

Nine-year-old Minerva Mint lives in Lizard Manor, an old, run-down mansion that sits on top of Admiral Rock, near the village of Pembrose in Cornwall, England. When Minerva was just a baby, her parents left her in a suitcase at the Victoria train station in London. Fortunately, Geraldine Flopps, an energetic custodian, found her, and the kind-hearted woman has taken care of her ever since.

Minerva wants nothing more than to find her parents, but it isn't easy. She only has a few clues, which were left with her in the suitcase: a volume of the Universal Encyclopedia, *a letter addressed to a certain Mr. Septimus Hodge, and the deed of property to Lizard Manor, complete with a lizard-shaped wax seal. For years, she has been trying to unveil the mystery herself, but now, finally, she has help: her new friends, Ravi and Thomasina.*

Her friends were with her when she found a mysterious box hidden in a kitchen wall at Lizard Manor. Inside the box, there was a small flute, and when it is played, hundreds of owls gather. The lid is engraved with a round tower and two words: Ordo Noctuae, *which means* Order of the Owls. *These words became the name of the young friends' secret club. They also have a hideout — a tower identical to the one on the box — and one goal: solving the mystery of Minerva's origins! The problem is, while Pembrose seems to be a quiet place, something always happens that requires their urgent attention . . .*

CHAPTER 1

THE PERFECT TRAP

Ding! Ding! Ding! A bell went off furiously.

"Get me down right now!" yelled Ravi. "You know I don't like to be up this high!"

He dangled upside down from a tree branch, his face just a few feet from the ground. The only thing keeping him from hitting the dirt was the rope tied around his foot.

"Hurray, it worked!" yelled Minerva.

Ravi frowned. He didn't share his friend's excitement. Actually, he was pretty upset. He crossed his arms and grumbled, "So, will you get me down now?"

"I told you it would work," said Thomasina, ignoring him. She showed Minerva the book she was holding and pointed at a page. "It's exactly like the picture, don't you think, Minerva?"

"Hey! I'm starting to feel sick. I'm warning you," Ravi said.

Minerva peeked at the page. "Hmm . . . it really is identical," she agreed. "But in the picture, the victim is suspended over a hole full of poisonous snakes."

"Unfortunately, there are no poisonous snakes in Cornwall," said Thomasina with a sigh.

Enough is enough! thought Ravi. "That's it! I've had enough of this!" he yelled. "The trap works. Now get me down!"

The girls looked at each other.

"What do you say? Should we free him?" asked Thomasina.

"Well, if *we* don't do it, he'll end up staying there forever," said Minerva, looking around.

There was absolutely no one else who could help him. They were in Bodmin Heath Moor, the wildest and most isolated place in Cornwall.

Across the horizon, all they could see were hills covered with purple heather and shrubs with yellow flowers. The wind was so strong that it seemed like it was trying to sweep everything away until only gray boulders remained. There were few paths and no homes, only ruins and an abandoned mine. The only things that lived there were some sheep and wild ponies, along with ducks, migratory birds, and frogs.

"The two of you, stop talking and get me down!" yelled Ravi, twisting and turning like a fish.

"Not if you use that rude tone," said Thomasina.

Ravi shot her a mean look. All those two did was argue. A few days ago, Thomasina had had this crazy idea to build all the traps she could find in her favorite adventure books. "We have to protect our hideout," she had said. Ravi thought it was a good idea at first, but he didn't realize that he would have to test every single trap.

Actually, they had let fate decide. For each trap, Thomasina had held three blades of grass in her fist, one of them shorter than the other. The problem was that Ravi always grabbed the shortest one.

"I've had enough of your traps!" the boy complained.

They had tried every kind of trap you could think of: trapdoors, snares, holes dug in the ground and covered with branches and leaves . . .

Minerva felt like she had to say something to restore the peace. "You know that we have to defend ourselves from Gilbert's gang," she told Ravi. "He's gone now, but he'll be back soon and we'll be ready."

"And he's not the only one we have to worry about," added Thomasina. "The Order of the Owl's hideout must be completely secure."

"Fine, then you're going to test the next trap!" said Ravi. "I'm done with it."

Thomasina put the book away in the elegant purse she always carried. Then she pulled out a pair of scissors and cut the rope around his foot.

"No! Wai—" started Ravi. But he couldn't finish

before falling to the ground. Luckily, a big heather bush softened the fall.

"You did that on purpose!" he yelled angrily as he stood up.

Thomasina straightened her shoulders stubbornly. "I thought you wanted to be freed," she said.

"How about a snack?" Minerva suggested before they *really* started to fight.

The countryside air and exercise had made them so hungry that Minerva's suggestion had a magical outcome: their squabbling stopped.

Before heading back for something to eat, they put the rope back where it was and tied a bell on it. Then they fixed it to the ground with a release mechanism that would go off if someone walked on it. If that happened, they would have captured a potential intruder!

They started toward their hideout, the round tower that peeked out over the first hill. It was called Owl Tower, maybe because of the engraved owl with big, round eyes on top of the entrance door.

"Let's race to see who gets there first!" said Minerva. The open space of the heath moor always made her feel like running.

"Okay!" shouted Thomasina, starting to sprint.

"Hey, that's not fair! I haven't said go yet!" yelled Minerva. She took off and soon passed her friend.

Ravi, on the other hand, just kept walking, rubbing his bruised bottom every now and then. He watched his crazy friends.

Minerva was in the lead. As she ran, she yelled and moved her legs like a wild animal. She was quite athletic: she ran, climbed trees like a squirrel, swam like a fish, and rowed effortlessly. She had taught herself how to do everything, and she knew how to get out of every situation.

Nothing scares her, not even the fact that she doesn't have her parents anymore, thought Ravi, watching her messy red hair bounce as she ran.

Thomasina didn't let Minerva get too far ahead, though. Ravi couldn't figure out how she managed to run in her fine summer dress and patent leather shoes. But she was as fast as the light and always perfect and elegant, without a stain or even a wrinkle on her dresses.

"First!" yelled Minerva, throwing herself on the ground in front of the tower's entrance.

* * *

The three friends had proudly furnished their new hideout to perfection. The ground floor was still bare, but once they climbed up the steep, little stone steps, they found themselves in a place of total comfort. They had brought everything they needed on their bicycles: sleeping bags, flashlights, an oil lamp, binoculars, windbreakers, extra pairs of rubber boots, and a first aid box. Minerva had also made them each a slingshot, just in case, and they had supplies to sweep and clean the place as needed.

"Ah," Ravi said with a sigh, falling on one of the colorful pillows that covered the floor. They were made out of velvet and soft silk. Thomasina had swiped them, one by one, from her fancy house.

"Bread and cheese for everyone?" asked Ravi, opening the picnic basket where they kept the food. His friends sat down next to him, and they spread creamy cheese on big slices of wheat bread. They ate greedily and drank cranberry juice.

Piles of Thomasina's adventure books and old copies of the daily newspaper, the *Cornish Guardian*, were scattered around them. An old, antique radio broadcasted local radio stations. Their favorite station was *Pirate FM*, which broadcasted funny news. While they enjoyed their snack, the radio filled the tower with happy music.

All of a sudden, the music stopped. A serious voice came on and announced: *"The famous outlaw Cain North escaped Darkmoor Prison last night. Be careful; he is very dangerous. Citizens, be warned. Do not approach him. And now the weather forecast . . ."*

Minerva turned the radio off and looked at her friends. She had cheese all over her face. "Hey, I recognize that name!" she said. "It was on the newspaper that Mrs. Flopps was reading this morning."

Thomasina pulled a copy of that day's *Cornish Guardian* out of her purse. On the first page, in capital letters, was the name *Cain North,* along with a picture. "You're right, that's him!"

"Wow, he looks evil," said Ravi with a shiver.

Thoughtfully, Minerva looked at the picture. "Darkmoor isn't far from here," she said. "I wonder if . . ."

Thomasina's face lit up immediately. "Are you saying that this could be a new mystery for the Order of the Owls?" She clapped her hands. "We could catch him and take him back to the police!" Her lovely face, surrounded by blond hair, looked excited.

She had been quite bored lately. They had gotten their hideout all set up, but they hadn't made any progress in solving the mystery of Minerva's origins. They had examined all of the clues from the suitcase a hundred times, but with no result. They were simply stuck.

Ravi was pale as a ghost. "Are you really thinking about chasing after dangerous criminals now?"

Minerva looked tempted. "Maybe we could . . ."

"No way!" yelled Ravi. "Didn't you hear what the radio said? He's a *dangerous* outlaw."

"It's better than doing nothing, don't you think?" said Thomasina. She couldn't stand even one day without an adventure. She stared out the window, as if waiting for the dangerous outlaw to appear and save her from her boredom.

The view from the top of the tower was wonderful. To the west were the Atlantic shore and Tintagel, the castle of the famous King Arthur. To the east were the High Moore dark hills with Brown Willy, the highest point in Cornwall. It was a five-hour walk away. To get there, you needed water, windbreakers, and good shoes.

"Oh, I wish something interesting would happen," whispered Thomasina.

And then something interesting did happen! *Ding! Ding! Ding!* A bell rang furiously.

Thomasina spun and looked at Minerva. "It's our trap!"

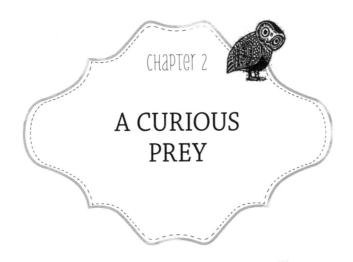

CHAPTER 2

A CURIOUS PREY

"Wait! We need to be careful and make sure it isn't anything dangerous!" Ravi yelled. His friends were already charging down the stairs. They didn't respond. They weren't even listening to him.

"What if it's the escaped outlaw?" Ravi shouted. "What will we do?"

Instead of stopping them, his words made Minerva and Thomasina run even faster. They seemed to have wings on their feet!

But when they got to the trap, the girls were disappointed. To tell the truth, even Ravi felt let down.

There was no one trapped in the rope.

"I don't understand. The trap went off," said Thomasina. She examined the rope hanging from the branch.

They searched for tracks.

"Someone stepped on the mechanism," said Ravi, examining the soil.

"Hey, look here!" Minerva called to them. She pointed at something black hiding among the heather under the tree. "Someone lost this."

They all took a closer look at Minerva's discovery.

"A tricorne hat!" said Thomasina, surprised. The hat had three tips and was very elegant. It was black with gold threading.

Characters often wore tricorne hats in the books Thomasina read, but she had never seen one in person. She took it from Minerva.

"People used this type of hat at least three centuries ago," she said.

"What's this?" asked Minerva, pointing at something on the front of the hat.

"It looks like a skull," said Ravi, "with crossed bones . . ."

"Like the pirates!" interrupted Thomasina. "The Jolly Rogers!" She gasped. "Guys, this looks like a . . . like a pirate hat! Look, there are some initials, too."

Two letters had been sewn inside the lining: *B. B.*

Minerva grabbed the hat and examined it. "A

pirate's tricorne hat," she said in a serious tone. "But how did it end up in our trap?"

They all looked at each other a moment and thought about it.

Thomasina was the first to break the silence, "Yes! A new adventure!" she shouted.

Minerva joined in her enthusiasm. "The Order of the Owls is back in action!"

Ravi shook his head and accepted his fate: nothing would stop his friends now.

"What's better?" he mumbled, following the girls. "A dangerous outlaw or a pirate ghost?"

Luckily, the two girls were so excited about the discovery of the tricorne hat that they forgot to reset the trap. *Well, at least we aren't at risk of capturing another dangerous adventure*, Ravi thought.

* * *

The sun was setting, and the heath moor was hard to navigate in the dark. Furthermore, Thomasina couldn't be late for dinner: her parents, Sir Archibald and Lady Annabella, expected dinner to be served at seven o'clock sharp every night.

So they decided to go home and made arrangements to meet up again the next day. They also decided that Minerva should keep the tricorne hat at her house.

"Let's meet at Lizard Manor tomorrow," suggested Minerva. "We could search our library for mention of a pirate with the initials *B. B.* What do you think?"

"Perfect. I can't wait!" said Thomasina.

"Okay," said Ravi with a sigh. He was never too happy about going to Lizard Manor. That big, broken-down house gave him the shivers.

Their three bicycles leaned on the backside of the tower, concealed with pieces of heather so that no one could see them from afar. Minerva put the hat in her bike basket and jumped on. The others climbed on their bikes and for the first half, they rode carefully because there was no real path to follow.

When they got to a crossroad with four different paths, they separated.

"See you tomorrow!" yelled Minerva, waving. She started pedaling as fast as she could toward Admiral Rock, while Ravi and Thomasina went toward the town of Pembrose, where they lived.

Minerva loved going fast, and she liked to think that her red bike was a rocket. But it was dangerous to ride with such speed in Cornwall. First of all, the climbs were steep and the ground was

bumpy. The roads were winding, with sudden turns. You could find yourself off the edge of a cliff in a heartbeat, with only air between yourself and the water! But that was why Minerva loved riding so fast: it was exciting, her heart pounded, and she felt like she was flying.

Despite being a wild biker, she had a surefire way to avoid running into people when she rode. She would simply yell, "Out of my way!" at the top of her

lungs. Then she would scream like a siren, so that everyone in her path moved immediately.

Well, almost everyone . . .

"*Watch ouuutt!*" shouted Oliver, the local policeman. On a bike himself, he swerved to miss Minerva and fell into a bush.

"Oh, no!" Minerva stopped, let her bike fall to the ground, and ran to see if her victim was okay.

No need to worry: Oliver was a big guy with a square jaw and the muscles of a boxer. Nothing could hurt him. But his bicycle wasn't so lucky.

"Minerva Mint, how many times have I told you not to ride so fast?!" he said, trying to straighten his handlebars.

"I'm sorry," she said. "But I tried to warn you. Didn't you hear me?"

Oliver rubbed his head with his hand. He was prematurely losing his hair, and everyone in town thought it was because of this nervous habit.

"Well, I was a little bit distracted, to tell the truth," he admitted. "You probably heard that a dangerous outlaw escaped from Darkmoor Prison. Well, I was investigating . . . looking for traces on the ground. I was doing what I'm supposed to do, so to speak," he said, inflating his chest proudly.

"Oh, I see," said Minerva, trying to keep a straight face. As far as she could recall, there had never been any criminals in Pembrose — not even a chicken thief. Oliver was the most bored and frustrated cop in all of Cornwall. Of course, he now looked thrilled about the possibility of a dangerous fugitive in town.

He flexed his muscles and clenched his jaw. "If he shows up here, I'll catch him," he said seriously. "I'm the terror of all outlaws. No one can run from me!"

Minerva started to feel a familiar tickle, and she covered her mouth with her hand to avoid laughing out loud. She wasn't sure why, but whenever someone lied to her, it felt like a feather was tickling her toes.

Knowing that the policeman didn't need her help, she got on the bike and left before she accidentally laughed in his face. "Bye, Sherlock Holmes!" she yelled.

CHAPTER 3

CORNWALL'S TERROR

To many people, Lizard Manor seemed quite creepy. From its spot on top of Admiral Rock, it looked as if it was about to dive into the foaming ocean. It was huge, with fifty-five rooms, and you could see it from miles away. Unfortunately, it was not well preserved, and Minerva and Mrs. Flopps expected it to fall on them any second. The first things to fall would likely be the high chimneys where fourteen owls made their nest.

One of the owls, the biggest of all, flew back and forth in front of a window on the third floor. It seemed like it was trying to figure out what Minerva was doing. The girl kept leaning out of the window, looking for her friends.

"They're late, Augustus!" she told the owl. "Do you see them?"

The bird landed on the windowsill and looked at Minerva. He moved his head suddenly, as if he was surprised.

Minerva's appearance that afternoon was even more peculiar than usual. She wore a black tricorne hat with an outfit to match. Minerva never bought any clothes, because she found plenty of them in the chests and closets of the mansion. (Of course, that's why she was always dressed in the most unusual way!)

This time, her clothing was completely over the top: she wore a white shirt with fluffy sleeves, a silk vest with red and yellow stripes, big knee-length pants, a dark blue jacket with maritime symbols sewed in gold, and tall boots that came up to her knees. A red scarf circled her waist and a wide belt sat across her shoulder. She also wore an earring in one ear, and around her neck was the chain with the small flute that called owls. Her flute was always with her.

Noticing Augustus's curiosity, Minerva removed her hat in a maritime greeting. "So, am I or am I not a perfect pirate?"

The owl's answer was to grab the hat and fly away.

"Oh, no!" she yelled. "Give it back!" She ran out of the room, flew down three sets of stairs in near darkness (the electricity did not work properly), fell on the last step, almost bumped into several paintings that were drying at the entrance, and popped into the yard.

"Augustus!" she yelled, shaking her hands toward the owl. He flew in circles around her head. "Please, give me my hat back!"

The owl let it fall right on top of Minerva's red hair.

"That was perfect!" shouted Minerva in admiration. "Thanks a lot!"

Ravi and Thomasina had arrived just in time to see the whole thing. They were still on their bikes, looking at the owl in shock.

"How did he do that?" asked Thomasina.

"He dropped it from at least sixty feet!" said Ravi.

Then they noticed Minerva's funny outfit.

The boy was speechless, while Thomasina let the bike fall and went to look at her friend.

Minerva turned around. "Nice, huh?" she said proudly.

Thomasina was clearly envious. "Do you have one for me as well, by chance?" she asked, lowering her blue eyes to the elegant, but boring, dress she was wearing.

Minerva grabbed her by the arm. "Let's go and find out!" She also grabbed Ravi's elbow and dragged him toward the entrance.

Ravi was always nervous to go inside Minerva's house. From the first day he had visited, while making a delivery for his mom, who managed Pembrose's post office, he'd tried to avoid the place as much as possible. After all, he hated lizards, and the name of the house made him very suspicious.

* * *

Minerva took her friends upstairs. Ravi kept his eyes low, both to watch his step in the dark and to avoid the haughty and threatening eyes of Minerva's ancestors, whose paintings hung on the walls.

Minerva led them into several rooms, where they searched chests until they both found an outfit of pirate clothes similar to Minerva's. They chose pants, shirts, and boots in their sizes. Then they changed their clothes so that they could do their library research in proper style.

Minerva spent her mornings studying at a desk that sat in front of a window facing the front yard. She didn't attend the local school, because her guardian didn't support public education.

The wooden desktop was covered with old volumes bound in leather, and the mansion's deed of property, with its lizard-shaped seal, sat atop a bookstand. Minerva kept it there so that she could easily study it and look for clues.

From the window, Minerva could watch Mrs. Flopps's garden. Some days, the old woman put on a big apron and pulled weeds from the flowerbeds as if she were in a trance. But soon, the sea or sky would awaken her artistic soul, and she'd run to gather her canvas and brushes. She sold her beautiful seascapes (along with delicious homemade jams) to tourists to earn a living for her and Minerva. It was enough money to survive, but not enough to repair the home.

Minerva had already carefully selected several big books on pirates, including *History of Piracy in Cornwall*, written by a local historian. They decided to start with that one, taking turns reading. They sat down in a circle on the old carpet in front of the fireplace.

Ravi read first. He flipped through the pages, looking for something interesting. After a while he said, "Hey, did you guys know that during the eighteenth century, this area was filled with pirates?

Here, there's a list. Let's see . . . aha! *B. B.* could be the initials of Black Bart, Cornwall's Terror!"

Thomasina grabbed the book from his hands, and Minerva read aloud over her shoulder.

"The cruel Black Bart is one of the most important figures of the golden age in piracy," she read. *"As a young man, he boarded Spanish ships in the Caribbean Sea and lived in Tortuga. When he was around forty years old, after accumulating a considerable amount of wealth, he came back to his home country and established his base in Cornwall. He became the chief of a very dangerous gang of outlaws based in . . . Pembrose!"* She paused and exchanged a look with her friends.

Minerva leaned in more. "It says that they were called the Ravagers of the Sea."

Even Ravi was fascinated. Now their three heads touched and three pairs of eyes stared at the page.

"It sort of seems like almost all the people in Pembrose were pirates or smugglers back then," said Thomasina.

"Yep, no one did honest work around here!" said Ravi.

Thomasina kept reading. *"Black Bart was like a king and the Ravagers his noblemen. He loved luxury and elegant clothing. He wore earrings, gold necklaces, and rings. Even the handle of his sword was made of gold, as was the stock of his gun, which he kept inside a red silk scarf. He carried so much gold on himself his chair had to be reinforced to support the added weight. But he was not refined at all. He burped at the table, even in front of important guests. If he didn't like a man, he made the individual walk across a boardwalk on top of Dragon Tooth, a spur of rock overlooking the open sea, and forced him to jump up and down by threatening him with his sword. The victim generally fell on the rocks below."*

"Whoa!" said Ravi.

"Keep reading!" said Minerva, completely mesmerized by the story.

Thomasina turned the page. *"According to legend, Black Bart became so wealthy that he built a City of the Ravagers, where he stored his riches. Some people think the city is on the mainland in the heath moor, while others think it is underneath Pembrose. Some even think that it is at the bottom of the sea. No one has ever found the entrance, which is why it is considered only a legend. Black Bart, after committing more bad deeds than any other outlaw in Great Britain, was cap-tured when Her Majesty's Crown decided to put an end to piracy. He was punished with a death sentence and hung, together with his mates, at the pennant of a ship."*

The three friends sat there in silence, soaking in the details of the chilling and exciting story.

"Anything else?" asked Minerva after a while.

Thomasina scanned the page again. "Hey, there's a footnote from the author here, and . . . I can't believe it!" she said, widening her eyes.

"What?" said Minerva.

"Yes, what?" echoed Ravi.

Thomasina looked at them and then, with a loud, clear voice, she said, "I think Black Bart is an ancestor of the Bartholomew sisters."

"No, that can't be!" said Ravi.

"Let me see," added Minerva.

According to the book, *Bart* was short for *Bartholomew*, the famous pirate's family name. It was unbelievable, because Gwendolyn and Araminta Bartholomew were the most delicate and nicest people in Pembrose. They lived at the Rose Villa, the nicest cottage in town. They owned the only fashion store in town, Bon Ton, where they sold hats, dresses, and other clothing that they created themselves.

"Wow," mumbled Ravi. "The Bartholomews are the descendants of a ferocious pirate."

Minerva looked at him. "Yeah, but the most important question is, what was the hat of a ferocious, three-centuries-dead pirate doing in our trap?"

"We're not sure that the hat really belonged to Black Bart," Ravi pointed out.

"Well, not *yet*," admitted Minerva. "That's why we have to investigate!"

"Right!" agreed Thomasina.

Suddenly, the delicious smell of freshly baked

scones tickled their noses. They followed the smell to living room number three (there were five living rooms at Lizard Manor), where Mrs. Flopps had set up a snack for them. They spread fresh butter and strawberry jam on the scones and shared them with the six foxes that lived among the room's couches. While they were eating, the Order of the Owls talked about the mystery of the pirate, and that made the snack even better.

CHAPTER 4

ALTHEA'S CURSE

The next day, Minerva was supposed to meet her friends after school in Pembrose. She sped along the winding roads on her bike, slamming on her brakes when she reached the school.

Classes had just ended, and Ravi and Thomasina were waiting for her at the entrance on their own bikes. The two students were in the same classroom and sat next to each other. Ravi had fallen in love with Thomasina Crowley on the very first day of school, just after he had moved from India. His love for her had helped him from being homesick, but it had also caused him some trouble.

"Hi. Did you bring the tricorne hat?" Thomasina asked Minerva.

Her friend pointed to the basket, which held a newspaper-wrapped package. "There it is. Let's go see the Bartholomews right away!" They had decided that the first step in solving the mystery would be to ask the sisters about their famous ancestor.

They zipped in front of the port, where anchored boats bobbed in the water. In the distance, a regatta was being held, a common sight for the area. The sea struck against a rocky beach full of lobster pots and nets, while an old fisherman took his chances on the dock.

It was just the beginning of June, but tourists wearing shorts, T-shirts, and sandals wandered the steep and winding roads, walking by sweet cottages with straw roofs and white walls. They took pictures and bought souvenirs. During that time of the year, many of Pembrose's residents changed their homes into bed and breakfast inns, so they could earn a little extra money after the bad winter season of fishing.

"It's odd to think that this village was once full of dangerous pirates, isn't it?" said Ravi, looking around. When he first moved there, Cornwall had seemed like a very boring place!

All of a sudden, Oliver appeared in front of them. His face was flushed, and he seemed distracted, like the last time Minerva had seen him.

"Like fugitives aren't enough!" grumbled the young man, stopping to dry the sweat from his forehead with a napkin. "Now I hear that some people think they saw a pirate wandering near their homes."

The friends held their breaths and looked at one another.

"They expect me to come running, like I have nothing better to do!" the policeman complained. "But what can I do? One thing is sure: I've got no time to waste with you three!" With that, he left on his bike, pedaling furiously with his strong calves.

"Did you guys hear that?" whispered Thomasina.

"Yes. This is becoming more and more of a mystery," said Minerva.

Ravi, who got pale just from hearing the word "fugitives," was thankful that they were just looking for a three-centuries-dead pirate. It sounded much better than looking for a living fugitive. *Or maybe not,* he thought, feeling doubtful all of a sudden.

When they reached Bon Ton, they left their bicycles outside the door. The small store was also a tourist office in the summer — the Bartholomew sisters were experts in local history — so the store was busier than usual. They had to wait while the sisters gave information to an Argentinian couple visiting Cornwall for the first time.

As they looked around the store, the three friends realized that something was wrong. The walls looked like they needed painting, and water was dripping from the ceiling onto some mannequins.

"What can we do for you?" Gwendolyn asked when the two Argentinians finally left.

"Would you like a cup of tea?" added Araminta.

The sisters couldn't look more different from each other. Gwendolyn, the oldest, was so tall that with her elaborate, blond up-do she almost touched the wood beams of the ceiling. In contrast, Araminta was a short, plump brunette.

To avoid being impolite, the three friends said yes to tea, and Araminta began making it. After talking about the weather and the tourist season, Minerva finally decided to ask the question. "We're very interested in the history of local pirates," she started. It wasn't even a lie. "Can you tell us anything about it?"

"Oh, we're experts on piracy!" said Gwendolyn. "You know, like today, Cornwall was a poor region even in the eighteenth century. It was home to simple fishermen and miners. People throughout the region began earning extra money by smuggling illegal items. There are many tunnels underneath Pembrose that were used to take banned items from the coast to the land."

"It didn't take long to go from smuggling to piracy," continued Araminta. "Since the coast is sloping and full of secret places, pirates could easily find places to hide and escape the English navy's controls."

"It was the golden age of piracy," Gwendolyn said with a sigh. She was getting lost in the story. "Ships full of treasures came from America and the Caribbean. Whole coastal communities specialized in plundering at sea. Or they raided ships that had sunk during thunderstorms. Or worst," she added lowering her voice, "they sank the ships themselves."

"Have you ever heard of the Ravagers of the Sea?" asked Araminta.

Minerva nodded. "We read about them in a book about the history of piracy."

"The Ravagers were the worst of them all," continued Gwendolyn. "They didn't just ravage the ships that sank naturally. They made them sink with tricks." She walked to a small window, threw it open, and told them to come closer. She pointed at a high spur of rock on the left of the port. "That cliff up there is Wind Peninsula. You can see for miles up there." She pointed to the cliffs below. "You see, it overlooks the Shipwreck Bay and the Perilous Rocks."

"The Ravagers drew in the ships that they wanted to sink. Then they killed all the survivors that tried to swim to shore," explained Araminta. "No one survived to bear witness to what had happened."

The friends shivered. The story was getting creepier by the minute.

"But . . . how did they do it? How did they draw the ships in?" asked Ravi.

Gwendolyn closed the window. For a second, she kept looking at the sea through the glass, then she invited them to sit around the table for their tea. "With *false lights*," she answered. "The Ravagers hung a lantern on top of a pole and reflected the light with mirrors so that it looked like a lighthouse. The ships would lose their route and crash against the rocks. Those ships were deliberately drawn into danger from lights that looked like they were pointing to safety. Instead, the lights made the ships sail directly into the cliffs."

"That's horrible!" exclaimed Minerva.

Gwendolyn poured another cup of tea to calm down a small tremor on her hand and poured one for her sister, too.

Minerva took advantage of the moment to ask the thing she cared about the most. "We, um . . . we read that the leader of the Ravagers was named Black Bart. Was he. . . well, was he your ancestor?"

The sisters blushed and exchanged an embarrassed look over their cups of tea.

Gwendolyn took a long sip. "It's true, Black Bart was the leader," she answered, putting her cup on the table. "And, yes, he was our great-great-uncle. That old shipwreck in the bay, the *Falconridge* . . . he personally made it sink," she added, sighing. "He became so cruel that not only did he attack ships in the sea, like he did in the Caribbean, engaging them in a fair duel, but he drew them into traps with false lights. It is said that he accumulated an amazing treasure."

"Which he kept in the City of the Ravagers!" interrupted Ravi.

"Exactly," answered Araminta. "But neither the city, nor the treasure, were ever found."

"And Black Bart, in the end, got a severe punishment for his wrongdoing," concluded Gwendolyn, lowering her eyes. "The gallows."

The three friends exchanged a series of silent messages: it was the right time.

Minerva stood up and said, "Excuse me for a second." She went outside to grab the tricorne hat she had left in the basket. She took it out of the newspaper and solemnly gave it to Gwendolyn. "We found this in the heath moor," she told her.

Astonished, the woman looked it over, and then gave it to Araminta.

Minerva cleared her voice. "There's some initials inside. *B. B.*"

The sisters looked closely at the lining.

"I can't believe it!" said Gwendolyn.

"It really looks like the same hat," mumbled Araminta.

"Come and see," said Gwendolyn. She led them

to a heavy curtain framed by two mannequins and pulled the rope.

The curtain opened to reveal a painting. It showed a pirate wearing a black tricorne hat with gold stitching and a skull at the front. The hat was identical to the one that Gwendolyn held in her hands.

"Please meet Black Bart," she said.

The famous pirate looked terrifying. The tricorne hat cast a shadow on his face, which was already dark from his beard, mustache, and big black eyebrows. He was wearing gold earrings, and even one tooth was made of gold. His eyes sparkled with cruelty.

They stared at the painting for a few minutes. Gwendolyn was the first one to talk. "Did you really find this hat in the heath moor?" she asked.

Minerva nodded. "Two days ago," she answered. There was no need to mention the trap and Owl Tower. Those were things that no one was supposed to know about.

Ravi was very pale. "But . . . this means that it belongs to the ghost of Black Bart!"

Thomasina was absolutely thrilled. "We're tracking down a pirate!"

Minerva looked at the sisters. They were quiet and looked pale and shaky.

Then Araminta looked up at her sister. "It's all our fault," she whispered.

"*Shhh*," said Gwendolyn, giving her a warning look.

But her sister would not stop. "It's because of the curse. I'm certain."

"What curse?" Minerva asked immediately.

Gwendolyn shook her head, but she realized it was too late.

"There's a legend in our family," she said slowly. Talking about the legend was clearly a huge effort for her. "Black Bart was a mischievous man. He did not value friendship nor honor. He didn't know what loyalty was. No one was safe with him, not even his mates," she explained. "You see, the Ravagers of the Sea were a group of ten men, plus a beautiful, charming lady. People claim she had special powers."

"What do you mean?" asked Ravi.

Gwendolyn went to grab the guide for the small, local history museum. She put on the glasses that hung around her neck. "Here she is. Her name was Althea. This is her portrait. The real thing is displayed at the small museum by the port, down at Fishermen Circle."

The three friends stretched their necks to see better. Althea did not look more reassuring than the captain of the Ravagers. Her hair was purple-black, like heather at night, and her eyes were big and dark, like the bottom of a well.

"Bewitching eyes," said Gwendolyn, following their gaze. "At the beginning, Black Bart was very much in love with her. Then he started to become jealous of her power and charm. He feared she wanted to take his place, so he got rid of her. He reported her as a criminal to British authorities. When the guards came to take her away to the Tower of London, Black Bart watched the scene with his usual bossy air. They had already handcuffed her wrists and ankles, when she turned, pointed at her enemy, and pronounced a terrifying curse."

The three children were completely fascinated by the story.

"What curse?" asked Minerva again.

Gwendolyn, very pale, pointed a finger and spoke as if she was Althea cursing the pirate. "*Black Bart, when it is your turn to go to the world of the shadows, your descendants will be persecuted with bad luck until you do at least one good deed!*" she said in a dramatic voice. Then she lowered her arm, and the color returned to her face.

"But how . . . if he's dead . . . ?" asked Thomasina.

With that question, the sisters looked really embarrassed.

"Might as well tell them everything," whispered Araminta.

Gwendolyn nodded. "Well, you see, Althea left a diary with a spell to evoke spirits. It's in the museum archive, along with documents of other local people, and . . ."

" . . . we used it! We used the spell!" concluded Araminta. Her hands had started to shake again.

Gwendolyn blushed. "As a justification, I can only say that we were moved by desperation. You see, we've had some very bad luck lately." She pointed at the water dripping from the ceiling. "The water pipes broke, deliveries were lost, and, above all, business is bad. We are at risk of losing the store," she said. "We have no way to pay the mortgage that is due in a few weeks." Gwendolyn paused. She looked as if she were about to cry.

Araminta continued for her. "So we remembered that old legend, and we decided to try to evoke our great-great-uncle to ask him to do a good deed and free us from Althea's curse. That way, maybe, all of our problems will be solved."

Gwendolyn felt a bit better. "It seemed like no big deal, because how would the ghost of a mischievous pirate do a good deed?" she said with a forced smile.

Araminta put one hand on her arm. "And we were sure it wouldn't work, but . . ."

"Maybe it did," ended Minerva.

"Someone saw Black Bart wandering the streets in the night," said Thomasina. "Oliver just told us."

The sisters looked like they were about to cry again.

"Oh, no! It's all our fault!" said Gwendolyn.

From the concentrated look in her green eyes, you could tell Minerva was thinking. She looked at the tricorne hat that Gwendolyn had set on a small chair. "Now I'm certain: Black Bart is back!" she said.

Everyone's eyes turned to the tricorne hat.

Araminta squeezed hard her sister's hand. "Oh, my goodness," she said. "We've really stirred up some trouble!"

Chapter 5

THE LONE
PIRATE INN

The following day was Saturday, so there was no school. Ravi, Minerva, and Thomasina went to visit Pembrose's history museum overlooking the port.

Other than the volunteer museum attendant, the place was empty: tourists preferred the landscape. The museum consisted of just one hall with portraits hanging on the walls, cases of boating and fishing instruments, and shelves of books and documents gathered by amateur historians like the Bartholomew sisters.

"There she is . . . Althea!" said Minerva, pointing at a painting.

"Wow, she looks even scarier than in the book!" said Ravi.

Feeling like the woman's black eyes were constantly watching them, they looked for her diary among the documents on the shelves. The small book had yellow pages and was stained with humidity and mold. The words that the Bartholomew sisters had used to evoke Black Bart were there, written in a pointy handwriting that was hard to read. The rest of the diary was filled with stories about the Ravagers' adventures and curses to start thunderstorms or control the sea.

"Even her writing gives me the chills," said Ravi, closing the diary. "She must have been a horrible woman."

"And powerful," said Minerva. "Maybe she was the one who caused thunderstorms, calling the ships toward the coast where they would follow the false lights and crash."

"So you think the legend is real?" asked Thomasina.

Minerva nodded. After all, in Cornwall, the line between what was possible and what was not was very thin.

After putting the diary back, they said good-bye to the attendant, a fisherman with a dark and wrinkly face who spent his time at the museum reading fishing magazines, and they left.

They were headed toward the dock where they had left their bikes when they crossed paths with Oliver.

The policeman's uniform was wrinkly, and he looked very nervous. His habit of rubbing his hair seemed to have gotten worse.

"You know, someone started the rumor that the pirate wandering our streets is the ghost of Black Bart, one of the Bartholomew sisters' ancestors!" he said with a nervous laugh. "But who?" He shook his head and went away mumbling, "Like I don't have enough to do. Fugitives, ghosts, pirates . . . I really need a vacation!"

The three friends went to sit at their favorite place, the little wall overlooking the sea. It was almost midday, and a light breeze blew across the water.

"Did you guys hear?" said Ravi. "Now everyone is talking about the ghost of Black Bart." In a small town like Pembrose, rumors spread fast.

"Yep, but no one has captured him yet," said Minerva. "So we're going to do it."

"Yes!" Thomasina agreed. She pulled the hem of her nice dress back so that it would not get wet.

Ravi looked at them both. He was about to say something, but he gave up. Nothing could stop those two.

Minerva threw a flat stone on the water, and it made five jumps. Her red hair was even messier than usual. That was always the case when she had a mystery to solve; she spent so much time thinking that she didn't have time to brush her hair. "Black Bart had vast riches from his piracy," she started, "but it was never found. We have to talk to the ghost and make him tell us where it is. Then we can return it to the descendants of the original owners. It will be a good deed, and we will free the Bartholomew family from the curse," she said. "Easy, right?"

"Very easy," agreed Thomasina.

Ravi could no longer remain quiet. "But . . . even Gwendolyn said it: why would the ghost of an evil pirate want to do a good deed?"

Minerva's green eyes sparkled with a mischievous light that the boy, unfortunately, knew too well. "Because I will convince him!"

Thomasina opened her purse and pulled out a map of the area, spreading it on her lap. "I've highlighted the places the Bartholomew sisters mentioned: Shipwreck Bay, Perilous Rocks, and Wind Peninsula. The trail to the top starts here," she said, pointing to a spot on the map not far from the dock.

"Perfect," said Minerva, getting up. "Let's go!"

"Now?" asked Ravi.

Minerva put her hands on her hips. "If not now, when? The mortgage on the sisters' shop is due in a few weeks. We can't waste any time!"

"Come on, lazy. You'll see . . . we'll get to the peninsula in a heartbeat," said Thomasina, jumping on her pink bike with her usual grace.

Ravi looked up toward the high rocky wall starting from the left of the bay. "Yes, it's nothing, right?" he mumbled. "Just a tiny little climb, that's all!"

* * *

They climbed a trail that could barely be seen, full of rocks and holes overlooking the sea. The sun and clouds were chasing each other in the sky, and the soft breeze turned into a wind that came in sudden gusts. Luckily, Minerva and Ravi had brought waterproof hoodies with them. The coats were good protection from the wind. Meanwhile, Thomasina wore a light cloak over her dress.

They explored the peninsula, which seemed to change according to the weather. When the sky was low and gray, it looked dark and lonely, but as soon as the sun was shining, it displayed a million colors . . . purple, pink, and yellow of the flowers, emerald green of the grass, silver of the granite, and turquoise blue of the sea.

Minerva and Thomasina pedaled like crazy, and Ravi feared that one of them would suddenly fall off a cliff into the sea. But luckily, after the first moments of euphoria, they slowed down to check the map and find the places where the Ravagers of the Sea had roamed. They went all the way to Dragon Tooth, the northern part of the peninsula, overlooking the open sea. Leaving their bicycles on the grass, they looked around.

"Can you imagine Black Bart making his enemies walk on a wooden boardwalk, poking them with the tip of his sword?" asked Thomasina, carelessly leaning forward to look at the rocks below.

Ravi followed her gaze. The cliffs were sharp like a shark's teeth. Afraid of heights, he moved back.

Minerva, on the other hand, liked to look down, taking in the salty air on her face and the squeaky calls of the birds flying around.

Thomasina pulled her binoculars out of her

elegant purse and held them to her eyes. She looked like a pirate searching for prey. "Hey, you can really see the remains of the *Falconridge* from here!" she said. She handed the binoculars to Minerva.

Minerva looked at the mast surfacing from the water. "I wonder if there was treasure onboard."

"Yeah, maybe Black Bart took it and brought it to the City of the Ravagers," said Thomasina enthusiastically.

Minerva looked at the sea with desire. "And where is the City of the Ravagers?" There was an endless stretch of possibilities in front of her.

Ravi kept his distance from the edge of the cliff. "Maybe we don't need to look that far," he said. "The city could be underneath the peninsula."

Thomasina put the binoculars away. "Come on, let's go, I know you don't like to be this high up," she said, winking.

"That's not true!" Ravi protested. "I mean, we can see plenty of places from here . . . and there's nothing."

He was embarrassed that the girl he loved thought he was a coward, but there was nothing he could do about his fears.

They kept exploring until their stomachs started to give warning signs: lunchtime was long past!

They decided to stop and rest by an old, abandoned house.

"It must have been an inn," said Ravi. "See, the sign is still there."

A wooden sign was moving in the wind, squeaking in an unpleasant way. They could still see the image of a coach and the letters faded by the weather: The Lone Pirate Inn.

The door was boarded shut with slats of wood. They walked all around the building to see if there was another entrance, but they just found windows with closed blinds. In front of the door, there was a trapdoor with a rusted, broken lock that no longer closed. They opened the door and looked inside with the help of a flashlight. It was just an empty room where rum boxes were kept once. The floor was several feet below, and they couldn't get in from there.

They decided to rest on a wooden bench by the door, huddling together to warm up. The wind had become crisp. They were so hungry, but unfortunately they did not have much food: just some small

ham sandwiches that Ravi had grabbed from his mom's store. They ate them in a heartbeat, without feeling satisfied at all. Their bellies were still empty when they smelled something delicious. Then an old man wearing a fisherman's hat appeared.

"Oh!" said the stranger. "I didn't know I would find anyone here. Usually there's no one around."

The three of them weren't listening to him; their attention was on a package of fish and chips that peeked out from the basket he was carrying.

"I come here for lunch when I can," explained the fisherman. Then he realized that they were staring at the basket as if they had not eaten in days. He smiled and said, "I fried more fish than usual today. Do you want some, perhaps?"

"Of course!" exclaimed Ravi.

Thomasina poked him with her elbow. "Yes, please, you're so kind," she said apologetically.

"Yes, please, and thank you so, so, so much!" echoed Minerva, trying to imitate Thomasina's perfect manners.

The man sat down with them to divide the fish. When they opened the wrapping, the fish was still crisp. It smelled irresistible.

For a while, they were too busy chewing to carry on any conversation, but when they were finished, the fisherman asked, "What are you guys doing here, anyway? This is no place for kids."

"We wanted to take a little trip," started Ravi. He realized that Minerva had already started to laugh, so he added, "You know, we like mysterious places." That was the truth.

"Well, you came to the right place then," said the man, serious. "Maybe it's not too scary during the day, but don't come here when it's dark," he warned them.

"Why?" asked Minerva, interested.

"Because you might see weird things," the old man answered. "Bad people used to hang out here, you know, and you can still feel their presence. I live in a small house not that far away from here, down the trail. I've been hearing weird sounds lately, footsteps in the night. I came all the way up here once to check things out, and a shadow with a tricorne hat and cloak appeared before me."

"Really?" asked Minerva, curious. "When did that happen?"

"A few days ago," answered the fisherman. "And at night, I saw lights on top of the peninsula," he added, shaking. "It was around midnight."

The Order of the Owls looked at one another. Minerva wanted to ask more questions, but they were hit by a gust of strong wind.

The man stood up, worried. He licked one finger and held it up to detect the direction of the wind. Then he shook his head. "The weather is changing. A thunderstorm could be coming," he explained. "I have to go get my nets out. Good-bye, children. For your own sake, don't stay here too long," he said, concerned. And he walked away down the path toward Pembrose.

Minerva's eyes sparkled. "Did you guys hear what he said? He saw a light on the peninsula."

"And a shadow with a tricorne hat," added Thomasina.

Minerva's cheeks glowed with excitement. "I think it's Black Bart who keeps doing bad things, like when he was alive."

Thomasina clapped her hands. "So the sisters really did manage to evoke him! It's really him!"

Minerva, sitting on the bench with her legs crossed and her hair crazier than ever, appeared thoughtful. "The old fisherman saw the lights at midnight. That means that tonight we must come back here and catch Black Bart by surprise," she concluded.

Ravi, who was silently listening to his crazy friends, jumped up from the bench. "You want to come back here at midnight?" he yelled, anxious.

"Of course. There's no other way."

"You heard yourself. The fisherman warned us to stay away from this place when it's dark!"

"Don't worry, we'll have our flashlights," said Thomasina.

"The weather's getting bad," Ravi tried again.

"There could be a storm." He looked at Minerva. "And if Black Bart has started up with his mischief again, how can you convince him to do something good?"

Minerva threw her red hair back with confidence. "I have my ways," she answered mysteriously. "Come on, let's go get ready." She climbed on her bike. "We have a long night ahead of us!"

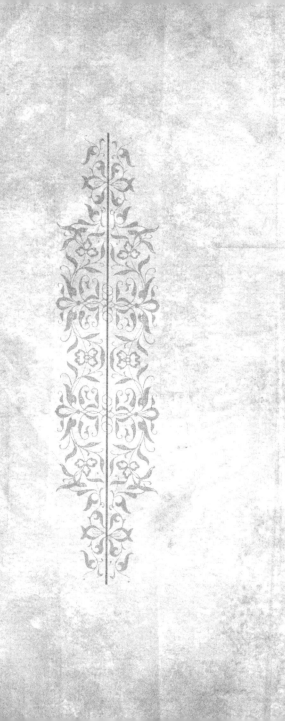

CHAPTER 6

A DARK AND STORMY NIGHT

It was a very long night for Ravi — the longest of his entire life.

Things actually started out surprisingly well: the wind was not as strong, and they didn't have school the next day, so losing a few hours of sleep would not be a problem. Ravi had told his mom that he was spending the night at Minerva's. Since the mansion had something like thirty-one bedrooms, Mrs. Flopps would never even know if they were there or not.

Thomasina, on the other hand, had put pillows

under her blanket so that it looked like she was lying under it. She had learned that trick in a book. In the story, the main character then climbed out of a window using the bedsheets, but Thomasina chose to go through the front entrance to be quicker.

The three friends met in front of Fisherman Circle at ten o'clock and started to climb Wind Peninsula, one bike after the other. Unfortunately, there was no moon, and when they were halfway there, the wind started blowing again. They were forced to leave their bicycles behind and walk.

"Are you girls sure you don't want to try another time?" yelled Ravi. The wind barked and the clouds lowered. The sea was wavy, and in the bay, big waves with foaming crests fell violently on the cliffs.

Ravi was about to repeat the question, thinking they had not heard him, when Minerva raised her hand. "Be quiet!" she yelled. She pointed toward Dragon Tooth. "Look, the light!"

"But it's not midnight yet," protested Thomasina, upset by the lack of punctuality.

Minerva, on the other hand, started to run. "Let's hurry! We have to get to Black Bart!"

Finding the right path in the dark was not easy, and if that was not enough, a thick fog was rising from the sea. It almost seemed solid, since the rays from the flashlights couldn't pass through it. Then the wind suddenly died down, and an eerie silence surrounded them.

The fog combined with the silence was too much for Ravi. "The fisherman was right," he whispered, shaking. "Something bad is coming."

But his friends kept climbing. Minerva was leading, and she told them, "Come on, it can't be far!"

Suddenly, another wall of fog came from the night and blocked them. They couldn't see even a foot in front of them. They held each other so they wouldn't get lost and stood side by side, shaking.

"What are we going to do now?" whispered Ravi.

Minerva looked around, trying to see something. "I'm sorry," she said, sighing. "I don't know where we are."

They stood still and held each other's hands, terrified by the idea of being swallowed by the fog. Then their ears picked up muffled sounds: steps, exclamations.

"Black Bart!" whispered Minerva. "He's getting away!"

"He doesn't seem far," whispered Thomasina.

The girls couldn't resist. They began walking, with Ravi following, toward where the noise was coming from. The steps now sounded like hammers.

But it was almost impossible to know where to go. Suddenly, they all tripped on a pile of rocks, and their flashlights fell, rolling away. They heard them fall and break on the cliffs below. Meanwhile the sounds of the steps were getting further away.

"Oh, no! We're at the edge of the peninsula," said Minerva. "Come on. We have to get back."

They kept fumbling, walking blindly and guiding themselves with their hands. But it felt like the sea surrounded them; the darkness seemed full of waves.

For an instant, a small break in the fog showed them a slice of sky, and they realized they were on the edge of a cliff that fell to the sea. Then the white mist closed around them again.

Ravi was paralyzed with terror. "We can't move, or we'll fall."

Thomasina pulled the compass from her purse to figure out which way to go.

Minerva, who was used to taking care of herself and could smell danger better than her friends, motioned to Thomasina to put her compass away. "We don't need that," she said. "Just one wrong step and that's it."

Ravi held onto his friends. He could feel his heart in his throat. "I knew this would happen," he said.

Minerva did not lose her courage. "We just have to stay still until the fog clears," she explained. "The only problem is that if the weather doesn't change, we run the risk of staying here all night and all day tomorrow." She was familiar with the fog rising from the sea. It was sneaky and deadly dangerous.

"Someone will come looking for us at some point," objected Thomasina.

"No one knows that we're here," Minerva reminded her.

Thomasina shivered. The fog was icy cold.

Ravi realized that his friend only had a light cloak on over her cotton dress. "Take my jacket," he offered.

"No way!" she said, proudly. The heroes in her books were always tough girls.

A bit upset from Thomasina's refusal, Ravi said, "We can't stay here. If we fall asleep, we'll fall down."

Minerva agreed. "You're right. We have to find a safer place."

Ravi looked at Thomasina, who was chattering her teeth. He felt a spirit of chivalry grow inside him. *I have to do something. I'm the man, after all*, he thought. . . . *Or maybe not.*

He clenched his jaw and tried to hide his fear. He wet his finger, like the fisherman did. The wind was coming from the east, so that was where the fog was coming from, too. And they knew that the fog rose from the sea. "Perfect," he said softly. "So we'll go left."

"What did you say?" asked Minerva, confused.

Ravi did not answer. He bent over, gathered some small stones, and put them in his pockets. "Follow me!" he said. He grabbed Minerva's hand. "I'm going first. Minerva, you hold onto me. Thomasina, grab Minerva's other hand."

His tone was so confident that his friends obeyed.

Ravi threw a stone on the left and heard it fall on the ground. Then he moved carefully. "Do exactly what I do," he warned the girls.

They kept walking that way for a long while that seemed to never end. The boy would throw a stone and then make a few steps in the same direction. He used his hands as well. All of a sudden, he yelled, "Stop!"

They found themselves in a gap among the rocks, away from the wind and sea. There was enough room for them to all lie down. "Let's stay here and rest," Ravi decided.

They huddled close to each other to stay warmer, and after a bit, they fell asleep. It was a terribly long night.

* * *

At sunrise, a loud *"Woot! Woot!"* woke Minerva up. The girl rubbed her eyes and stretched. She looked around and saw that it was a beautiful day and the fog was gone. Then she saw Augustus, looking at her with his big, round yellow eyes sitting on top of a rock in front of her.

"Good morning, Augustus!" she greeted him happily. "Did you come to look for me?" She stood up and realized that they had almost reached the base of the peninsula the previous night without even realizing it. The spot where they slept was very close to where they had left their bicycles in the heather.

"Wow, we almost made it back!" she told the owl. "As you can see, we're fine. You can go back home."

Augustus suddenly moved his big feathery head, as if he wanted to say, "Okay." He hooted once again and flew away, his wings moving gracefully. Shading her eyes with one hand, Minerva followed his slow flight towards Lizard Manor. Then she took a deep breath of the salty air and moved her legs and arms energetically — something she did every morning to activate the blood circulation. "Wake up, lazies, wake up!" she yelled, nudging her friends.

"Huh? What?" mumbled Ravi.

"Where are we?" asked Thomasina, opening her eyes.

"It's morning! We must get back home before they realize we were ever gone!" Minerva said, shaking them.

Ravi sat up suddenly. "It's daytime!?" he said in shock.

"And we're safe and sound thanks to you," Minerva told him with a smile.

Thomasina sat up and looked at him. "My hero . . ." She sighed and gave him a loud kiss on his cheek.

To Ravi, it was like an electric shock. "What? Eh? Oh!" he babbled, blushing. He touched his cheek with one hand, blushing even more, and looked around in despair. "Well, there are our bikes!" he said. "What are we waiting for? Let's go home!"

CHAPTER 7

FALSE
LIGHTS

That afternoon, Minerva, Ravi, and Thomasina met in town to go talk with the Bartholomew sisters. But when they got to Bon Ton, it was full of tourists. There was even a huge line outside the door.

"Well, how can we get in now?" asked Minerva.

"Fools!" a voice said behind their backs. "They believe a ghost pirate is wandering the area, and they're curious to see his descendants!"

They turned and saw Oliver. This time, he was wearing his police suit and hat, which covered his very little hair. He carried a suitcase, as if he was about to leave.

"Where are you going?" asked Minerva, curious.

Oliver puffed up his chest, making his jacket a bit tight. "I got a tip," he answered. "Someone saw Cain North around Boscastle. I'm leaving for a few days to go look for him. Don't need cops to look for ghosts." He shook his head at the tourists. "Now, if you'll excuse me, I have something to do." He climbed in his car, and before leaving, he leaned out the window. "I won't be around to protect you guys, so behave!" he yelled, stepping on the gas.

"He really is a terrible cop," Ravi said.

Minerva, in the meantime, couldn't stop giggling: Oliver showing off always made her ticklish.

Thomasina, on the other hand, wanted a plan. "What are we doing now?" she asked. "We can't talk to the sisters. Should we go back to the peninsula?"

Minerva, who had calmed down a bit, shook her head. "It's pointless to go there during the day. And as for going there at night . . ." She looked at Ravi, who had already gone pale. ". . . I think we need a strategy first."

"I think we have to surprise Black Bart while he's making signs," objected Thomasina. "It's obvious that he's still very mean and is trying to sink ships like when he was alive."

"I'm not going up there again!" said Ravi.

Thomasina gave him a mean look. "But weren't you a hero?" she asked him.

He blushed. "You called me that —"

Minerva interrupted him. "I thought of something. Lizard Manor is situated right in front of Wind Peninsula, on the other side of the bay," she said. "It's in the perfect spot to watch for the light with binoculars. I could keep an eye out for it at night," she suggested. "I could try to figure out if the light always goes on at the same time or if something else happens. Then we'll have time to think of a plan. What do you guys think?"

"I agree," said a relieved Ravi. At least there was no immediate danger.

"Okay," mumbled a resentful Thomasina. She didn't agree, but she didn't have a better idea.

* * *

That same night, Minerva started her stakeout in her bedroom window on Lizard Manor's top floor. She wore her favorite pajamas, the ones with the matching nightcap with a big pom-pom that fell down her cheek. Thomasina's powerful binoculars sat on her lap.

Minerva's room, like the other thirty bedrooms in the house, was huge and full of spiderwebs, especially around the posts of the big bed. The webs there were never cleared because Minerva thought it was more practical to sleep in her sleeping bag in a tent on the floor. That way she never had to change the bedsheets.

The owls were taking turns keeping her company on the windowsill. They looked at her with tilted heads, surprised that she was up so late.

A slice of moon reflected a line of silver on the sea.

A salty breeze messed Minerva's red hair and tickled her nose.

Around midnight, right when the girl's eyes started to close, a light appeared up on the peninsula.

Minerva grabbed the binoculars, searching in that direction, but it was so dark that all she could see was the light going on and off for a few minutes. When it finally went off for good, she pointed the binoculars toward the water, but there were no ships around. There was nothing. Just the darkness of the Atlantic.

"Very mysterious," the girl whispered to the owl next to her. "I think that's all for tonight," she said with a big yawn. "Good night." She closed the window and dragged herself to the tent.

The following afternoon, in their hideout in the heath moor, she told her friends everything. Thomasina was tired of doing nothing. She insisted that they go back to Wind Peninsula. Ravi decided to go just because the sun was shining brightly. But they didn't discover anything new and ended up just

having a snack on the bench of the abandoned inn and returning home.

The next few days went much the same way: at night, Minerva observed the lights, and in the afternoon, she reported to the others at Owl Tower. She was so tired in the morning that she kept falling asleep during her studies in the library. She would nap with her head in a book until Mrs. Flopps yelled, "Lunch is ready!"

Then she'd wake up and, after eating whatever she had in her dish, she'd hop on her bike and go to Owl Tower, riding through the heath moor on her red rocket.

* * *

"I'm tired of this!" complained Thomasina, crossing her arms. It was almost a week since their nighttime trip to the peninsula. The girl was upset that they hadn't made any progress. "Weren't we supposed to have a strategy by now?" she asked Minerva.

They were in their tower, lying on the pillows. It

was so comfortable that, to tell the truth, Minerva had fallen asleep. "What?" she mumbled, waking up.

"Maybe it's not really Black Bart," Ravi tried to say. "It could be a reflection, or one of the natural lights that can be spotted every now and then in the heath moor. What do they call them . . . will-o'-the-wisp?"

Minerva was not convinced. "No, it's an artificial light. It goes on and off with the same intervals, more or less at the same time," she explained.

"So we have to go there at night again!" insisted Thomasina. "If we don't, how will we catch the pirate?" She stood up to emphasize her words, and a book fell from her lap. (She was so frustrated that she was trying to console herself by reading someone else's adventures.)

"What are you reading?" Ravi asked her. He hoped to distract her a bit.

Thomasina grabbed the book. "I started it yesterday. It talks about smugglers moving stolen goods from the coast to the mainland. Instead of meeting in person, they communicate with lights using a lantern and a mirror. They use a code called . . ." She flipped through the pages of the book to find the exact spot. ". . . It's right here. 'Morse code. The smugglers transmitted letters and numbers through flashing lights.'"

At those words even Minerva stood up. "What did you just say?"

Thomasina gave her the book, and Minerva read for herself.

"Oh, of course!" said Minerva, hitting herself on the forehead. "It was right there in front of my eyes." She started pacing back and forth as she read from the book. "The lights on the peninsula go on and off with regular intervals every night." She stopped. "Obviously, someone is trying to communicate using the Morse code, just like in this story!"

"Of course! Why didn't I think of that?" Thomasina said enthusiastically.

Minerva scanned the book. "Here it says that for a message to be transmitted by light, you use points and lines. A point corresponds to a light that doesn't last long, while a light lasting three times a point is a line." She looked around. "I need a piece of paper and a pencil!" she said, chewing her lip. "And a flashlight, too!"

Thomasina looked inside her purse. "Here you go," she said, handing Minerva everything she needed.

Minerva started to turn the flashlight on and off several times. With all her hard work and thinking, she messed her red hair up even more, so much so that it almost stood straight up on her head.

Like so many of her fantastic abilities, Minerva's memory was quite incredible. After a few attempts, she recalled the sequence. "Yes, I think it's this one: long light, short light, then one interval . . ." She drew a series of points and lines on the paper. "There it is!" She showed her friends what she had drawn.

⁻ . ⁻⁻⁻   ⁻ .⁻. . .⁻ ... ..⁻ .⁻. .

"Huh?" said Ravi, thoughtful.

At the bottom of Thomasina's book there was a table that showed which letters corresponded to the various combinations of lines and points. Minerva studied it. "It's two words," she decided. "The first, - . ---, means 'no'. While the second, - .-. . .- ... ..- .-. ., means 'treasure'."

"'No treasure!'" exclaimed Thomasina.

"The treasure of the Ravagers!" yelled Ravi.

"Hurray, it really is a message!" said Minerva, waving the piece of paper.

In celebration, they grabbed each other by the arms and danced around the room.

When they paused to catch their breath, Ravi said, "So if the light isn't used to attract ships, but for the Morse code . . ."

" . . . it means that someone is looking for the treasure, but hasn't found it yet," Thomasina finished the sentence for him. "And every night that someone is telling someone else that he didn't succeed."

Minerva was thoughtful again. "The problem now is . . . who is he trying to tell?" she said. "And who's the author of the messages? Black Bart?"

"But he knew where the treasure was," Ravi pointed out.

"Maybe he forgot after all this time," suggested Thomasina. "After all, it has been three centuries!"

Minerva started to walk around the room again. "One thing is certain. If they find the treasure before us, we're in trouble."

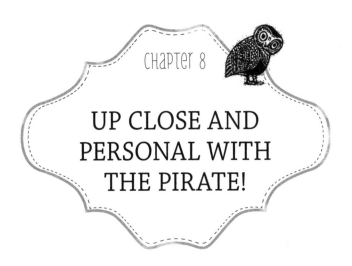

CHAPTER 8

UP CLOSE AND PERSONAL WITH THE PIRATE!

That night, what the three friends most feared happened.

Around eleven o'clock, Minerva went to the window to observe the light on Wind Peninsula. She had a notepad, a pencil, and Thomasina's book nearby. When the light appeared, the girl grabbed the binoculars and, to her surprise, she found that the message had changed.

"Huh, what happened?" she mumbled, moving her nightcap pom-pom, which kept falling in her eyes. She started drawing points and lines on the paper, and when the peninsula went dark again, she read what she had written. It said, "Found!"

"Oh, no!" she said, looking at Augustus, who sat on the windowsill. "They found the treasure!"

The owl blinked his yellow eyes, meaning that the situation was serious.

Minerva nervously pulled her pom-pom, unsure of what to do. "We must do something! But what?"

She knew she couldn't go to her friends in the middle of the night, so she crawled inside her sleeping bag, hoping to sleep. *That way I'll be ready when morning comes!* she told herself. But she was certain she would have trouble falling asleep.

She must have slept some, though, because Augustus woke her up an hour before sunrise. The owl bit the naked foot that peeked out from the yellow tent.

Minerva sat down. "What's happening?" she mumbled. She noticed Augustus and felt better. "Oh, thanks for waking me up," she said, still half asleep.

She slipped out of the tent and stretched a bit with her special moves. Finally she said, "I'm ready!"

Fortunately, it was Saturday. The girl got dressed quickly, putting everything on inside out. She slipped on her rubber boots as she went down the stairs and hurried into the yard, where her bike was waiting.

She was in front of Thomasina's house in a heartbeat. She started throwing little stones at her friend's bedroom window.

Thomasina appeared and leaned out of the

window, wearing a pink nightcap and some sort of clip on her nose. She had read in a book that a well-positioned clip would turn the nose upward.

As soon as she saw Minerva's expression, she knew that something bad had happened. "I'm coming down," she whispered.

In mere moments, she was downstairs, dressed in her perfect style, patent leather shoes included. She jumped on her pink bike and, while they pedaled toward the post office, Minerva told her what had happened.

About twenty minutes later, three bicycles were climbing Wind Peninsula. The sun was coming up behind the cliffs, but the world was still asleep and wet with dew.

It hadn't been easy to convince Ravi to join the expedition, especially after Minerva and Thomasina had sneaked through his window to wake him up. Ravi's room was on the ground floor, and he always left the window open a crack. Of course, he would now have to stop doing that.

When they were close to The Lone Pirate Inn, Minerva told them to stop.

"Look, someone's been here!" she whispered, pointing at the door that had been boarded up. "The door is halfway open."

Scared that someone would hear them, they hid their bikes behind some rocks without saying a word. Then they stood there, looking at the house, unsure of their next move.

"What are we going to do?" whispered Ravi.

"Should we go in?" whispered Thomasina.

A breeze blew, and the sign squeaked in a sinister way.

"Yes," decided Minerva. "Maybe we'll catch the person who makes the signals while he's asleep, and take him by surprise." To avoid giving Ravi the chance to complain, she immediately started walking toward the house.

Thomasina followed right behind her, and Ravi, sighing, went too.

Minerva opened the door a bit more. They quietly

stepped inside, and Minerva closed the door behind them. The window blinds were closed, so it was dark. Thomasina took the flashlight from her purse and turned it on.

They were in a big room covered in dust and spiderwebs. There was no one around. There wasn't much furniture: just a wood counter, tables, and chairs. Boxes full of empty bottles sat on the floor. A staircase, on the right side of the entrance, led upstairs.

Thomasina pointed the flashlight toward the floor. Minerva pointed at some big footprints in the dust that led to a big fireplace.

Carefully, they walked to the fireplace, putting their feet inside the larger footprints so they didn't leave traces.

Minerva looked at the fireplace. "It seems like it's leaning to the right," she whispered.

She told the others to help her, and they all pushed. The fireplace started to slide a bit toward the right, revealing a hole full of burlap bags.

They were so excited that they opened one, for-getting the danger.

"Wow, gold bars!" whispered Ravi. "We found the treasure!"

"Shhh!" said Minerva. "Listen."

She could hear someone walking on the rocky path leading to the inn. The footsteps sounded iden-tical to the ones on the peninsula on the night they were trapped by the fog.

"Someone's coming!" whispered Minerva. "Put everything back!"

They closed the sack, pushed the fake fireplace back to its position, and looked for a place to hide.

Thomasina pointed to the stairs. They followed the footprints once again, reached the stairs, and made it the second floor just as the front door opened.

The footsteps sounded very menacing. The three friends went to hide in a corner of a room with broken floorboards. From there, they could peek downstairs through the cracks. What they saw made them feel as cold as ice: there stood a pirate with a tricorne hat on his head! It was his big boots that made the chilling noises.

A man entered behind the pirate. He held a flashlight, which threw some light on the pirate's face. The three friends held their breaths, expecting to see a black beard and some sharp teeth. But it wasn't Black Bart, nor a ghost, but a man in the flesh. His black tricorne hat was identical to the one they found in the heath moor.

"There you are," he said.

He lifted a flashlight as well, and the three friends saw the other man's face. He was Cain North, the dangerous man who had escaped prison!

"So where is it?" North asked with a threatening tone.

"You could be nicer," the pirate complained. "After all I've been through, don't I deserve a thank you?"

Cain North got closer and grabbed the pirate's collar. "Listen here, Jim. I got no time to waste!"

The man called Jim went away, upset. "Look, I did all the work, while you were just sitting around, waiting for my signal!" he complained. "Who's the one that, since the day he got released from prison, worked in that stupid pub where people have to wear pirate's clothes?" he complained, slapping the tricorne hat. "I had to pay for this one myself since I lost the first one while I was looking for the treasure in the heath moor. I ended up in some poacher trap, and I ran so no one would see me. But I forgot all about the hat. They were mad about that at work, and I had to pay a fortune for a new one. They're tight at the Beautiful Brig!"

The children looked at each other. Beautiful Brig was a tourist pub in the town of Trewlin, a few miles from Pembrose.

"That's what *B. B.* stands for," whispered Minerva. "Beautiful Brig, not Black Bart!"

"So it's a coincidence that his tricorne hat is identical to Black Bart's?" said Ravi softly.

Minerva nodded and reminded him to be quiet.

"It wasn't easy to escape from prison either!" said Cain North. "They're looking for me; I had to hide."

"If only we could have gotten more information from that crazy Bill Gunn before I got out of prison . . . I could have avoided all this trouble," said Jim. "Unfortunately, he hasn't been the same since he hit his head when he tried to escape Darkmoor. He doesn't know where he is or what year it is. He thinks he pulled off the robbery of the century, even if it was sixty years ago. He calls the loot his treasure. One day he says it's in Bodmin Heath Moor, another day it's in Pembrose, then a tower, and last but not least, an inn. I haven't been sleeping at all, looking for the right place! I've spent all of my free time from work searching for old Bill Gunn's treasure, and I'm tired of it."

"All you do is complain!" said Cain North.

"Look, after giving you signals from the top of the peninsula one night, I ended up in a thick fog. I almost fell to my death!" said Jim resentfully.

The three friends exchanged another look. So, that was him that they'd heard in the fog!

"Do you think I had fun sitting in hiding, waiting

for your messages? We couldn't meet up, 'cause someone might see me. I'm sure the law is looking for me. And I'm sorry you had to use the lights to send me a message, but you know, unfortunately, they don't give us a cell phone when we escape prison," said Cain North sarcastically. He raised a fist as if to threaten Jim. "Now, enough with this chitchatting. Let me see the treasure! There's a boat waiting for us at the port, and we'll be able to escape abroad. But first I want to make sure you're not cheating me."

Jim laughed. "Oh, don't worry. The treasure is exactly like old Bill told us. And it's right in front of your eyes."

At that exact moment, Ravi moved and made the floor boards squeak.

The two men looked at the ceiling.

"What was that?" asked Cain North nervously. He walked a few steps toward the stairs. "Is there anyone upstairs?"

"No, this place has been abandoned for years. The door was boarded closed."

The fugitive didn't look convinced. "But you heard it yourself." He went up the first step.

Minerva, Ravi, and Thomasina crouched down closer to the floor and closed their eyes. They wished they were somewhere else.

The fugitive was almost halfway up the stairs when Jim called him back. "Come on, let's not waste any time! It's a rat." He looked around. "I can't get out of here soon enough. This place gives me the chills. I heard talk about a ghost."

"That's nonsense!" said Cain North. He gave a quick look up the stairs then he turned back. "But you're right, we've got no time to waste. Show me the treasure!"

The children started to breathe again and peeked through the hole. Their heads were close, their muscles tense.

Jim pushed the fireplace like they had, revealing the burlap bags. "Ta-daaa!" he said. "This is old Bill Gunn's treasure — the robbery of the century from the Bank of England!"

Cain North opened a bag and smiled in satisfaction. "So it is."

"What did I tell you? What do you want to do now?"

"You stay here on lookout. I'll prepare everything for us to leave. The boat's captain is an old friend of mine. I just have to assure him that everything is okay, then I'll be back here with a truck to get the gold bars to the boat."

"And how are you going to get that?"

"Steal it, of course. I'll be back in a couple of hours." He pulled up a hood so that it covered most of his face, and then he left.

Jim stayed there looking at the treasure for a bit, as if he could never get tired of the sight. Then he sat on a chair and yawned a couple of times. After a few minutes, his head started to nod. It wasn't long before he started snoring loudly.

"What should we do now?" whispered Ravi.

Minerva looked at Jim from the hole in the floor. "He's asleep," she said. "You heard him; he hasn't slept for days. Let's go down. If we're quiet he won't hear us."

"But . . . we can't leave the treasure here!" whispered Thomasina.

"Ugh, that Oliver," said Ravi in a low voice. "He left town while the fugitive he's gone looking for is right here! Even if we call him, he might not make it back in time."

Minerva stood up with her hands on her hips. She looked like a young warrior — like the Roman goddess Minerva herself. Her green eyes held a fighting spirit. "Oh, but we don't need him!" she said.

Her friends looked at her, surprised.

"We don't?" asked Ravi skeptically.

She put one hand on his shoulder. "At least not now," she said with a big smile. "Come on, let's go. I'll tell you everything when we get to our bikes." She grabbed him by the arm. "And don't worry, Ravi. I'm sure that an old, mean pirate will help us when the time comes," she added mysteriously.

CHAPTER 9

ON WITH
THE TRAP

Led by Minerva, who was pedaling as fast as she could on her red rocket, they got to Lizard Manor in a heartbeat. It was not yet seven o'clock, and Pembrose and its countryside were still asleep, like every Saturday morning. No one could have imagined the threat of two dangerous outlaws nearby.

After less than an hour, the three friends were back at the old inn, with everything ready according to Minerva's instructions. Their bicycle baskets held the black tricorne hat and some of the pirate clothes they had found in the chests at Lizard Manor. They also had some thin branches that they had gathered in the yard.

Minerva had whistled for the whole trip: it seemed like what was about to happen put her in a good mood. As they got off the bikes, Ravi looked at her. Was it really possible that she wasn't a bit scared? Thomasina was hopeless, because she really thought that life was just like in the adventure books. But Minerva had always lived by herself, and she could see danger.

Ravi wouldn't uncover anything by studying Minerva's face; he couldn't even see her face! She had applied a thick layer of Mrs. Flopps's anti-aging lotion. It looked like she was wearing a white mask, and all one could see were her eyes. She said that it was all part of her plan.

"Let's hope your plan works," mumbled Ravi.

Minerva's eyes held an encouraging smile. Then the girl checked her pocket to make sure an important part of her plan was still in place. Her hand touched a stone wrapped in a piece of paper. "Everything's fine," she said satisfied. "Let's proceed!" She was talking without opening her mouth to avoid ruining her lotion mask.

They approached the inn quietly. The door was half open, like they had left it. Minerva tried to look inside, and then she pulled her head back.

"Jim is still asleep in there," she whispered. "Come on, let's do this!"

They put their load on the ground and crouched in front of the trapdoor that was next to the main entrance. The wood boards closing the trap entry were rotten, so they got rid of them in no time, hiding them in the grass. Then they put some branches over the trap entry and covered the whole thing with leaves.

When they were done, Minerva looked over the result. She scratched her nose; the lotion was bothering her a bit. "A perfect trap," she decided. She winked toward Thomasina. "Thanks to your books."

"Are you sure it's going to work?" asked Ravi.

"I think it looks just as it did before," said Thomasina.

"And when Cain North comes back, he'll be in a hurry and won't stop and check," said Minerva.

They stepped over the trap and entered the inn, taking the pirate clothes with them.

Jim was still sitting on the chair, in the same position he was in when they left him; his head was reclined back and he was sleeping deeply with his mouth open.

They went upstairs and quietly got dressed. Minerva wore a white shirt with puffy sleeves, a vest, and a jacket that was ten times her size. She put on the tricorne hat. Ravi kept a T-shirt on, but changed his jeans for a pair of trousers that stopped at his knees, and added big boots. Thomasina, on the other hand, stayed exactly as she was, in her little, lacy dress.

"And now?" asked Ravi nervously.

"Let's wait," answered Minerva, trying to flatten her wild locks underneath the tricorne hat. "You'll see! It's not going to take long."

After a few minutes, they heard some footsteps outside the inn.

Alert, the three friends tried to listen more closely.

"Jim, it's me!" yelled Cain North from the trail. "I found a truck, but it can't get *heeeere*..."

There was a scream and a tumble.

"He fell in the trap!" whispered Minerva. "Come on, let's go!"

As decided, Thomasina climbed up on Ravi's shoulders, while Minerva, agile as a monkey, climbed on Thomasina's. Her pirate jacket was so long that it covered Thomasina completely once it was buttoned. Only Ravi's pants and boots were showing.

"Ready?" asked Minerva.

"Attack!" whispered Thomasina from underneath the jacket.

"Yes . . . let's go," Ravi said nervously.

"*UUUAAAHH!*" yelled Minerva.

"*UUUAAAHH!*" yelled Thomasina.

Ravi was too busy trying to walk down the stairs without falling to yell. He watched his step from the jacket's buttonholes.

Heavy steps sounded on the wood boards, and Minerva started to shake her arms in front of her like a real ghost. Minerva shook her arms in front of her like a real ghost. On her head, she wore the tricorne hat. Her face was white, and she grinned devilishly.

"*UUUAAAHH!*"

When he heard his friend tumble into the trap,

Jim woke up a bit, but he was still half asleep. Once he heard the moaning though, he stood up and found himself face to face with a huge pirate with a mean expression.

"Help!" the man screamed in terror, and without looking where he was going, he hurried toward the door.

The ghost chased after him, screaming, "*UUUAAAHH!*"

Jim was so scared that he fell in the trap, right on top of his friend.

The big pirate stopped on the edge of the trap-door. Minerva looked down and smiled at the two men. "Bye-bye, criminals!" she said, waving her hand.

Suddenly, they heard someone coming toward the inn, and Oliver showed up from the trail.

"Here's our police officer!" said Minerva.

"Finally!" mumbled Ravi. "We called more than one hour ago."

"Well, he got here just in time to get all the credit," said Thomasina.

"Come on, Ravi, let's get moving," Minerva told him. "You're our legs!"

Looking toward the inn, Oliver saw a terrible sight: there was a big pirate at the door, or rather, the ghost of a big pirate, with a pale face and mean look.

"Oh, my . . ." he said, stopping all of a sudden. His big, square jaw dropped.

The ghost smiled, bowed, and greeted him with a wave. Then he let something drop and disappeared behind the heather bushes behind the inn.

The police officer couldn't move for several

minutes. He shook off his shock only when he heard someone asking for help. Going to the trapdoor, he looked down and found two people scared to death.

He grabbed the object that the ghost had left. It was a stone wrapped up in a piece of paper. He unwrapped the paper and read:

Dear police officer,

These two people are the dangerous outlaw Cain North and his accomplice, Jim. Behind the fireplace, you will find Bill Gunn's treasure.

Your humble servant,

Black Bart

Oliver read the piece of paper once again, and then he rubbed his head. "Oh, wow . . ." he said, sighing. "The ghost does exist!"

CHAPTER 10

THE RAVAGERS OF THE SEA

On Sunday, the town of Pembrose was in an uproar. In the last twenty-four hours, their quiet, sleepy corner of Cornwall had seen a few things!

Now, in addition to tourists, journalists and photographers from the capital filled the streets. They all headed to the fashion store of the Bartholomew sisters, two local celebrities. A small crowd of curious people gathered around the store.

Gwendolyn and Araminta were at the entrance, smiling at the cameras. They were wearing identical dresses in pink silk, with puffy sleeves and lots of ribbons.

Ravi, Minerva, and Thomasina watched them from far away.

One of the journalists said, "Where's the cop that arrested Cain North? He'll need to pose for the camera as well!"

Oliver appeared from the crowd in a brand-new uniform. He was so proud that it looked like his new shirt was about to explode on his chest. His shoes were shining, and his hair was full of gel. "Where should I stand?" he asked, closing his jaw in a smile.

"Between the Bartholomew sisters!" another photographer yelled.

The two young women took the robust officer's arms. Tons of flashes went off, and the crowd cheered, "Bravo! Bravo!"

Gwendolyn, Araminta, and Oliver kept changing poses and smiling.

Minerva looked at them, amused. "They're having fun, huh?"

"They're stars now," said Thomasina.

Ravi looked a bit upset. "It's not fair, though," he said. "The Order of the Owls solves an important case, and that cop takes all the credit!"

"All we need to know is that we did what was right," Thomasina reminded him. "It's better. Remember, we're Pembrose's protectors."

"Yeah, but I can't stand him!" grumbled Ravi, glaring at Oliver as he flexed his muscles for the cameras.

The three friends had decided they wouldn't take the credit for catching Cain North and his accomplice, leaving it to Oliver and, above all, to Black Bart's ghost. That was why, when they called the police from Lizard Manor, before going back to the inn, they didn't mention their names and spoke with a big pirate's voice.

Oliver told everyone that the ghost of the mean pirate revealed where the outlaws were. He also directed them to the stolen money of a famous robbery at the Bank of England, accomplished sixty years earlier by an old man named Bill Gunn.

Minerva smiled in satisfaction. "Now Gwendolyn and Araminta think Black Bart did a good thing."

"And they think they're free from the curse," ended Thomasina.

The two sisters were radiant. Everyone wanted to see Black Bart's descendants, and their store was full of people. Business was great. If things kept going this way, they would easily pay the mortgage and save the store.

The laces and dresses sewed by Araminta and Gwendolyn's industrious hands had become so popular that the sisters even got orders from London! And there were articles not only in the *Cornish Guardian* but even in the *Times* of the dangerous pirate that served justice, with pictures of the two descendants posing next to the creepy portrait.

"I've had enough," said Ravi. "Let's get out of here!"

"Agreed," said Minerva. "There's still something we have to do!"

"Huh?" asked Ravi. He noticed that his friend's green eyes were sparkling with mischief, and he thought, *Oh, no, not again!*

Minerva didn't give him time to ask questions. She hopped on her bike and started climbing toward Wind Peninsula. It was a nice, sunny day, and a warm breeze came from the sea, blowing the grass, flowers, and Minerva's red hair. The girl pedaled as fast as she could, yelling, "Out of my way!"

Thomasina followed her just as quickly, but with more elegance. Her blond hair, tied with a nice blue ribbon, didn't move.

Ravi was a bit slower. He kept asking himself, "What is Minerva thinking?" But the day was so beautiful that he decided to enjoy the moment. "Hurray, the Order of the Owls has solved another case!" he yelled enthusiastically.

"Hurray!" his friends yelled to the sky and sea.

* * *

Minerva stopped in front of the old inn. It was the first time they had been back. The London police had come to take away Cain North and Jim. For a few hours, the house had been surrounded by a yellow ribbon, warning others to keep back. There had even been some officers from the Bank of England, the rightful owners of the treasure. They had really looked out of place on top of the bare peninsula, with their suits, hats, and umbrellas on their arms. But now they were all gone.

"What a shame . . . everything's over now!" said Thomasina, looking around.

"Well, who says that everything is over . . ." said Minerva, walking toward the entrance.

Ravi started to feel nervous again. "W-w-what do you mean?"

Minerva jumped over the trapdoor and pushed the front door. Good. It wasn't locked. She turned toward her friends. "You never know what you can find . . . if you know where to look." She winked and went in.

The blinds were open on the windows, so it wasn't as dark as when they were there before. The dusty floor was full of footprints, and the fireplace looked like an open mouth. The burlap bags were gone, and only an empty hole remained.

Minerva stepped closer to examine it.

"What are you looking for?" asked Thomasina, following her movements with curiosity.

The girl curled up her nose. "I don't know," she answered. "It's just . . . it's a pity that we couldn't find Black Bart's treasure . . ." The fireplace was so big that Minerva fit inside perfectly. She turned toward her friends. "I couldn't sleep last night. I just kept thinking about it," she continued. "I told myself that this place must have had a purpose before Bill Gunn used it for his treasure."

"You're right!" said an excited Thomasina. She entered the fireplace as well, but she was too tall and had to go back.

Ravi looked at them, his arms folded. "Let me remind you that the police have already been here."

Minerva's green eyes were shining. "I know, but . . . they weren't looking for anything. They only wanted to get the sacks with the gold bars back."

Thomasina looked at the fireplace. "So do you think that Black Bart's treasure is here?"

Minerva shook her head. "No, it's clearly empty," she said. "But there could be something else . . . something small," she explained. "A sign or a clue, for example." She put one hand on the brick wall, feeling her way upward. She stopped and looked at her friends.

"What?" asked Ravi.

"What have you found?" echoed Thomasina impatiently.

"There's something sticking out here, and something attached above it," mumbled Minerva. She stood on her tippy toes, and she almost disappeared. "Uh, it's stuck," she said. She pulled hard and fell on her back, raising a cloud of ashes. "*Achoo*! Ouch, that hurt!" she said.

"What is it?" Ravi and Thomasina asked her.

She immediately forgot about her pain. Minerva raised her right hand, revealing a small, wrapped package. The paper around it was old and dark from the smoke.

"Let me see!"

"Give it to me!"

The girl climbed out of the fireplace and opened the package. There was another package inside; a

sheet of parchment, closed with a big green seal . . .
in the shape of a lizard!

"Hey, it's identical to the deed of property to your
house!" said Ravi. He remembered exactly how it
looked; that's how scared he was of reptiles!

Minerva unrolled the paper, trying not to damage

the seal. "It's a portrait," she said, showing it to the other two.

It was a miniature painting with eleven people dressed as . . . pirates!

The three friends leaned in around the painting.

"There's Black Bart!"

"And there's Althea!"

"So . . . they must be the Ravagers of the Sea," said Minerva. "Do you remember what the Bartholomew sisters said? Ten men plus a woman."

Thomasina grabbed the portrait. "Look, there's a list of names on the back. Black B. is the first. Then, Althea V.," she read. "I haven't heard of the others . . . Merrival M., Hawksmoor N., Galloway F., Barlow H., Ashton L., Burke Q., Colington J., Chatterton O., Ravenswood W. Eleven names in all," she said.

They turned the small portrait again and looked at the faces of the Ravagers of the Sea, one by one.

"Wait, I've seen this one before!" said Minerva, pointing to a man with red hair under a tricorne pirate hat. His nose was hooked and his eyes emerald green. He was posing close to Black Bart and Althea.

Minerva tried to think. "Where have I seen him before . . .?"

"Well, you couldn't have met him in the flesh. He's been dead for the past three hundred years," said Ravi.

Minerva's face full of freckles smiled. "You're right. Now I remember. His face is hanging in the staircase at Lizard Manor!"

* * *

The staircase was the darkest place in Lizard Manor. The three friends, who were still short of breath from the ride over on their bikes, each took a candle (Minerva always kept several fresh ones at the entrance) and climbed the stairs. They shined light on each of the faces that stared at them from the walls.

"There it is!" said Thomasina. She held the candle high in front of a portrait.

"Yes, that's him," confirmed Minerva, standing up on her toes to see the painting better.

It was the same face, wearing a proud expression. The man had eyebrows as red as his hair. Instead of the black pirate tricorne hat, he wore an elegant feathery hat. His hair wasn't as wild as in the miniature painting. Here, it was tied in a ponytail according to the eighteenth-century fashion.

"You couldn't tell as much from the miniature, but you guys look alike," said Thomasina.

"Do you think so?" asked Minerva skeptically. She moved her eyebrows up and down. She did not think they were as snobbish as the ones of the man in the portrait.

"There's a name here," said Ravi, indicating the bottom of the frame.

"Merrival M.," read Minerva.

Thomasina extracted the miniature from her purse and went through the list of names. "There he is . . . Merrival M."

"So one of your ancestors was one of the Ravagers

of the Sea!" said Ravi. "You're a descendant of a pirate!"

The boy wasn't really that surprised. Now that he thought about it, there was something pirate-like about her. Maybe the way her eyes sparkled.

"Wow!" said Minerva, trying to get used to the news. It was hard to read her expression in the candlelight. Finally, she said, "Help me get this painting down!"

They set their candles down on the stairs and grabbed the heavy frame. As they took the painting down, they turned it around so Merrival's face was toward the wall. Minerva shined a candle near the back of the canvas. An envelope was stuck to the top right corner. She grabbed it and noticed that it also had the green lizard seal.

She held the envelope in front of them for a bit, pausing to take in the moment. Then Minerva opened it. Inside there was a piece of paper folded in two and a small golden key.

The piece of paper read:

When the owl is cut in half,

And the lizard loses its tail,

You have found the City of the Ravagers.

Go there now or it'll disappear in one hour.

"Wow . . . the City of the Ravagers!" said Minerva.

"And it says how to find it right here!" said Thomasina excitedly.

"But you can't understand a thing," Ravi pointed out.

Thomasina looked at him resentfully. "So you don't think we can figure out what it says?"

"Yeah, the tougher the better!" said Minerva, putting an arm around Thomasina's shoulder.

Thomasina was very excited. She looked at her friend. "You know what? One of your ancestors was one of the Ravagers of the Sea! That's why there were so many pirate clothes in your chests."

"So you own the treasure," said Ravi.

It was too much for Minerva to take. She blushed as if she was about to burst. "I can't believe it!" She turned the painting back around and looked at the face framed by red hair. It seemed to be in a staring contest with her. "Merrival M.," she said, like she was waiting for him to reply, "Yes?"

Minerva smiled. "I haven't found my parents yet,

but I know I have a relative named Merrival, who was a pirate!"

"Does the *M* stand for Mint?" asked Ravi.

Minerva shook her head. "I'm not sure," she answered. "Mint is the last name that Mrs. Flopps gave me when she found me in the Victoria train station. You know, before we came here, this house hadn't been lived in for so long that no one in town even remembered the name of the previous owners."

Or maybe they don't want to say their name out loud, thought Ravi with a shiver.

Thomasina lifted a candle and examined the other frames. "Mathilde M., Malcom M.," she read. "After the first names, there's always an *M*," she said. "Now that I think of it, even the first names all start with an *M*!" She continued to shine light on the portraits. "Mowbray M., Mylena M. . . . The initials are always double *M*."

"Like on the suitcase that Minerva was found in!" Ravi reminded them.

"Did you ever notice that before?" Thomasina asked Minerva.

Her friend shook her head. "It's always so dark here, since the electricity's never worked right," she explained. "I guess I've never read the names."

"Well, there's another clue to add to the mystery of your origins!" Thomasina said. She looked at Ravi.

He was excited, too. With this new discovery, the mystery of their friend's origins was more interesting than ever. Now the Ravagers of the Sea were part of it, and there was a fantastic treasure!

Minerva pulled the small golden key out of the envelope. It sparkled in the candlelight. The reflection glowed in the eyes of the three members of the Order of the Owls.

"Do you guys think this is the key to open the City of the Ravagers?" asked Ravi.

"Yes, one hundred percent for sure!" answered Thomasina. "Now we just have to solve the riddle and find the city . . . and the treasure!"

"And maybe we'll find out something about my parents!" said Minerva enthusiastically.

"First, I have a request. I need a snack," said Ravi. "I'm starving from that bike ride!"

"Okay, but let's hurry," Thomasina said. To tell the truth, she also wanted some of Mrs. Flopps's warm scones with jam. It was always better to face new adventures with something in the stomach.

Minerva was still looking at the small key. "You know what? The ghost of Black Bart has performed a good deed for the Order of the Owls as well."

And at that moment, the three candles went out, as if a ghost had spitefully blown out their flames!

WHAT CHARACTER ARE YOU?

Are you carefree like Minerva?
A bit nervous like Ravi?
Which character are you most like?
Take this quiz to find out!

1. YOU ARE OFF ON AN ADVENTURE. WHAT ARE YOU WEARING?

A. A tidy dress clothes, not even a wrinkle to be found.

B. An Indian dress or perhaps a pirate costume . . . whatever best suits the adventure.

C. A T-shirt, jeans, and tennis shoes. Who cares what it looks like, as long as I can move easily?

D. Something to protect me from the elements as I paint outdoors. All of my adventures take place behind my paintbrush.

2. IT'S A TYPICAL SCHOOL DAY. YOU ARE:

A. Secretly reading an adventure book. Nothing is more important!

B. Anywhere from the heath moor to the pier, it depends on what I'm studying But most of the time I'm in my library.

C. Sitting in my classroom at school, gazing at my secret crush.

D. Making jam and preparing fresh scones for teatime.

3. ALL OF YOUR FRIENDS ARE LEARNING TO DIVE OFF THE HIGH DIVE. YOU:

A. Can't wait to try. I am sure to do a perfect dive right from the start!

B. Are the one teaching everyone else how to do it. I can dive like a penguin.

C. Feel nervous. After all, I'm afraid of heights.

D. Will be there to take photographs of everyone. Maybe I'll get some beautiful shots.

4. YOUR FAMILY:

A. Is serious and proper, but they really love me and only want the best for me.

B. Is a little untraditional — friends and distant relatives mostly.

C. Is hardworking, running our family business.

D. Is small, but very loving.

5. YOUR IDEA OF A PERFECT DAY:

A. I spend the day searching for clues to reveal my latest mystery. I like to pretend I'm a hero in an adventure book.

B. After waking in a tent, I prepare for a day of tree-climbing, running, and swimming. I like to be active!

C. As long as I can stay away from trouble and enjoy some tasty things to eat, I'm happy!

D. I paint the day away, only taking a break to bake fresh scones.

6. YOUR DREAM VACATION IS:

A. Treasure Island, of course, to search for treasure, or perhaps just adventure!

B. Anywhere, if I could take the trip with my parents.

C. Somewhere hot and sunny. I love the sun.

D. To the mountains or the shore . . . as long as there is a beautiful view to sit in front of, I'll be happy.

7. YOUR BIGGEST PROBLEM IS:

A. Feeling bored. If I don't have enough excitement in my life, I start to feel down.

B. The meanest kid in town is out to get me!

C. I'm afraid of lots of things . . . including that someone will find out how scared I am.

D. My house is falling apart, bit by bit. Plus, there's an animal-control problem.

8. IF YOUR FRIENDS ARE IN TROUBLE, YOU:

A. Well, to be honest, I might have gotten them into trouble to begin with.

B. Use my clever mind and special powers to get them out of trouble as soon as I can.

C. Step up and get things back on track when needed, even though I'm not usually the group leader.

D. Might not even realize that something is wrong. I tend to live in my own little world.

9. YOU THINK ANIMALS ARE:

A. Precious creatures. We should protect them and make sure they are safe and happy.

B. Among the greatest friends around. I treat them as my equals, keeping lots of pets.

C. A little scary. I'm nervous around birds, woodland creatures, and especially lizards.

D. Absolutely lovely, especially in my paintings.

IF YOU CHOSE:

Mostly A: You are **THOMASINA**. Even though you are elegant and proper, you enjoy adventure above all else. Just make sure to stay safe!

Mostly B: You are **MINERVA**. You are active, with special gifts that don't come along every day. You love your friends and are a great protector of animals.

Mostly C: You are **RAVI**. You may be a quiet, timid person, but no one is as brave as you when needed. What a great friend!

Mostly D: You are **MRS. FLOPPS**. You are creative and a bit of a dreamer. You appreciate the beauty in things, especially your friends.

Elisa at age 3

As a child, I had red hair. It was so red that it led to several nicknames, the prettiest of which was Carrot. With my red hair, I wanted to be Pippi Longstocking for two reasons. The first reason was that I wanted to have the strength to lift a horse and show him to everyone! The second was that every night my mother read Astrid Lindgren's books to me until she nearly lost her voice (or until I graciously allowed her to go to bed). As I fell asleep each night, I hoped to wake up at Villa Villacolle. Instead, I found myself in Milan. What a great disappointment!

After all of Lindgren's books were read and reread, my mother, with the excuse that I was grown up, refused to continue to read them again. So I began to tell stories myself. They were serialized stories, each more and more intricate than the one before and chock-full of interesting characters. Pity then, the next morning, when I would always forget everything.

Elisa today

At that point I had no choice; I started to read myself. I still remember the book that I chose: a giant-sized edition of the Brothers Grimm fairy tales with a blue cloth cover.

Today my hair is less red, but reading is still my favorite pastime. Pity it is not a profession because it would be perfect for me!

GABO LEON BERNSTEIN

I was born in Buenos Aires, Argentina, and have had to overcome many obstacles to become an illustrator.

"You cannot draw there," my mom said to me, pointing to the wall that was smeared.

"You cannot draw there," the teacher said to me, pointing to the school book that was messed.

"Draw where you want to . . . but you were supposed to hand over the pictures last week," my publishers say to me, pointing to the calendar.

Currently I illustrate children's books, and I'm interested in video games and animation projects. The more I try to learn to play the violin, the more I am convinced that illustrating is my life and my passion. My cat and the neighbors rejoice in it.

Gabo

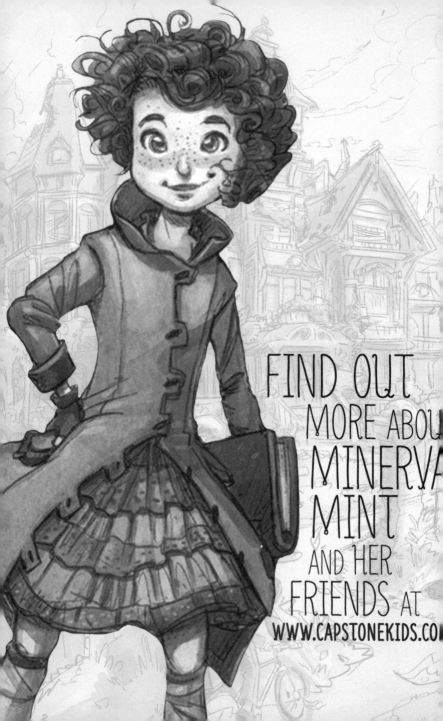

FIND OUT
MORE ABOU
MINERVA
MINT
AND HER
FRIENDS AT
WWW.CAPSTONEKIDS.CO